A Moose in a Maple Tree

The All-Canadian 12 Days of Christmas

Cover Design by Jennifer Harrington

Printed in Canada by Friesens

Library and Archives Canada Cataloguing in Publication

Townsin, Troy, 1975-
A moose in a maple tree : the original all-Canadian 12 days of Christmas / by Troy Townsin ; illustrated by Jennifer Harrington.

ISBN 978-0-9868892-3-3

1. Twelve days of Christmas (English folk song)--Adaptations.
2. Christmas stories, Canadian (English) 3. Christmas--Juvenile fiction.
I. Harrington, Jennifer, 1973- II. Title.

PS8639.O998M65 2011   jC813'.6   C2011-905389-6

Watch this book come alive and sing-along with the animated version on YouTube.

A Moose in a Maple Tree

The All-Canadian 12 Days of Christmas

By Troy Townsin
Illustrated by Jennifer Harrington

www.amooseinamapletree.com

On the first day of Christmas,
a Canuck sent to me
a moose in a maple tree.

On the second day of Christmas,
a Canuck sent to me
2 polar bears
and a moose in a maple tree.

On the third day of Christmas,
a Canuck sent to me

3 snowmen

2 polar bears

and a moose in a maple tree.

On the fourth day of Christmas,
a Canuck sent to me

4 totem poles

3 snowmen

2 polar bears

and a moose in a maple tree.

On the fifth day of Christmas,
a Canuck sent to me
5 hockey sticks
4 totem poles
3 snowmen
2 polar bears
and a moose in a maple tree.

On the sixth day of Christmas,
a Canuck sent to me
6 whales breaching
5 hockey sticks
4 totem poles
3 snowmen
2 polar bears
and a moose in a maple tree.

On the seventh day of Christmas,
a Canuck sent to me
7 beavers building
6 whales breaching
5 hockey sticks
4 totem poles
3 snowmen
2 polar bears
and a moose in a maple tree.

On the eighth day of Christmas,
a Canuck sent to me
8 lobsters nipping
7 beavers building
6 whales breaching
5 hockey sticks
4 totem poles
3 snowmen
2 polar bears
and a moose in a maple tree.

On the ninth day of Christmas,
a Canuck sent to me

9 mounties riding

8 lobsters nipping

7 beavers building

6 whales breaching

5 hockey sticks

4 totem poles

3 snowmen

2 polar bears

and a moose in a maple tree.

On the tenth day of Christmas,
a Canuck sent to me
10 salmon leaping
9 mounties riding
8 lobsters nipping
7 beavers building
6 whales breaching
5 hockey sticks
4 totem poles
3 snowmen
2 polar bears
and a moose in a maple tree.

On the eleventh day of Christmas,
a Canuck sent to me
11 sled dogs mushing
10 salmon leaping
9 mounties riding
8 lobsters nipping
7 beavers building
6 whales breaching
5 hockey sticks
4 totem poles
3 snowmen
2 polar bears
and a moose in a maple tree.

On the twelfth day of Christmas,
a Canuck sent to me

12 skiers skiing
11 sled dogs mushing
10 salmon leaping
9 mounties riding
8 lobsters nipping
7 beavers building
6 whales breaching
5 hockey sticks
4 totem poles
3 snowmen
2 polar bears
AND...

a moose in a maple tree!

This book is dedicated to the people of Canada and to all those who visit this wonderful country.

About the Author

Troy Townsin is a proud new Canadian!

Born in Melbourne, Australia, he worked as an actor and playwright before embarking on a round-the-world backpacking extravaganza taking him to several continents. Troy has had many jobs. He has been a Stage Manager in Australia, a Teacher-Trainer in Thailand, a Beverage Manager in the UK, an Information Officer for the United Nations and a Columnist for CBC radio in Canada. Troy has won several awards for his writing, including a prestigious "Travel Writer of the Year" award with TNT Magazine UK and a "Gourmand World Cookbook Award".

Troy fell in love with a Canadian girl, married her and then fell in love with Canada, his new home.

About the Illustrator

Jennifer Harrington is an illustrator and graphic designer who grew up in Vancouver, British Columbia. A trained anthropologist, she decided to follow her childhood passion for the visual arts.

She now lives in Toronto, Ontario, where she runs JSH Graphics, a graphic design company that specializes in corporate branding. Jennifer has illustrated numerous ad campaigns and worked as an art director on magazines in Vancouver, Toronto and London, England.

Others books by Troy and Jennifer:

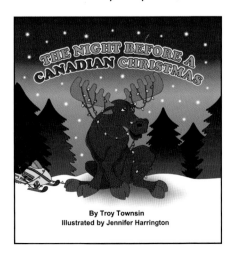

www.amooseinamapletree.com